THIS WALKER BOOK BELONGS TO:

_____

_____

_____

For Beth

*There are days when Bartholomew is naughty,
and other days when he is very very good.*

First published 1992 by Walker Books Ltd
87 Vauxhall Walk, London SE11 5HJ

This edition published 2008

2 4 6 8 10 9 7 5 3 1

© 1992, 2007 Virginia Miller

The moral rights of the author/illustrator
have been asserted.

This book has been typeset in Garamond.

Printed in China

All rights reserved

British Library Cataloguing in Publication Data:
a catalogue record for this book is
available from the British Library.

ISBN 978-1-4063-1186-0

www.walkerbooks.co.uk

EAT YOUR DINNER!

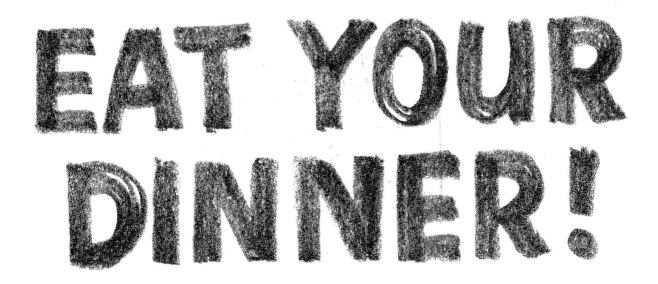

Virginia Miller

WALKER BOOKS
AND SUBSIDIARIES
LONDON • BOSTON • SYDNEY • AUCKLAND

George came looking
for Bartholomew with his dinner.
"Dinner's ready, Ba," he said.

"Have you washed your face and hands?"

"Nah!" said Bartholomew.

George said, "Sit up, Ba,

and eat your dinner."

"Nah, nah, nah, nah,

NAH!" said Bartholomew.

"Eat your

George said in a big voice.

Bartholomew ate one spoonful,

then he had a little rest.

George sat down at the table
and began to eat his dinner.

Bartholomew watched
until George had finished.

Then George left the table
and returned with a large honey cake.

He cut a slice and ate it and when
he had finished he took the rest away.

Suddenly Bartholomew thought,
Eat your dinner!

He thought of the honey cake…

with the pretty pink icing…

and the cherry on top...

and he licked his bowl perfectly clean.

He went to find George.

"Have you finished, Ba?" George asked.
"Nah," said Bartholomew, and George smiled
and gave him the slice of cake
with the cherry on top.

WALKER BOOKS is the world's leading
independent publisher of children's books.
Working with the best authors and illustrators
we create books for all ages, from babies
to teenagers – books your child will
grow up with and always remember. So…

FOR THE BEST CHILDREN'S BOOKS,
LOOK FOR THE BEAR